Dear Parents:

Congratulations! Your child is taking the first steps on an exciting journey. The destination? Independent reading!

STEP INTO READING® will help your child get there. The program offers five steps to reading success. Each step includes fun stories and colorful art or photographs. In addition to original fiction and books with favorite characters, there are Step into Reading Non-Fiction Readers, Phonics Readers and Boxed Sets, Sticker Readers, and Comic Readers—a complete literacy program with something to interest every child.

Learning to Read, Step by Step!

Ready to Read   Preschool–Kindergarten
• big type and easy words • rhyme and rhythm • picture clues
For children who know the alphabet and are eager to begin reading.

Reading with Help   Preschool–Grade 1
• basic vocabulary • short sentences • simple stories
For children who recognize familiar words and sound out new words with help.

Reading on Your Own   Grades 1–3
• engaging characters • easy-to-follow plots • popular topics
For children who are ready to read on their own.

Reading Paragraphs   Grades 2–3
• challenging vocabulary • short paragraphs • exciting stories
For newly independent readers who read simple sentences with confidence.

Ready for Chapters   Grades 2–4
• chapters • longer paragraphs • full-color art
For children who want to take the plunge into chapter books but still like colorful pictures.

STEP INTO READING® is designed to give every child a successful reading experience. The grade levels are only guides; children will progress through the steps at their own speed, developing confidence in their reading.

Remember, a lifetime love of reading starts with a single step!

For the best mom ever —K.L.D.

Published in the United States by Random House Children's Books, a division of Penguin Random House LLC, 1745 Broadway, New York, NY 10019, and in Canada by Random House of Canada, a division of Penguin Random House Ltd., Toronto.

Step into Reading, Random House, and the Random House colophon are registered trademarks of Penguin Random House LLC.

Visit us on the Web!
StepIntoReading.com
randomhousekids.com

Educators and librarians, for a variety of teaching tools, visit us at RHTeachersLibrarians.com

ISBN 978-0-385-38423-0 (trade) — ISBN 978-0-375-97347-5 (lib. bdg.) — ISBN 978-0-385-38424-7 (ebook)

Printed in the United States of America   20 19 18

By Kristen L. Depken

Illustrated by Tino Santanach

& Joaquin Canizares

Random House 🏠 New York

Barbie can be

a gymnast!

She is

on a team.

Teresa, Skipper, and
Summer are on the
team, too.

Coach Jenna is
their coach.

Coach *Jenna*

Barbie and her teammates
work together.

They get ready
for a big meet.

Barbie balances
on a beam.
Her team cheers!

Barbie dances.

She twirls a ribbon.

Barbie jumps.

She does a triple twist!

Oh, no!

Barbie falls.

Her team catches her.

Barbie asks

Coach Jenna for help.

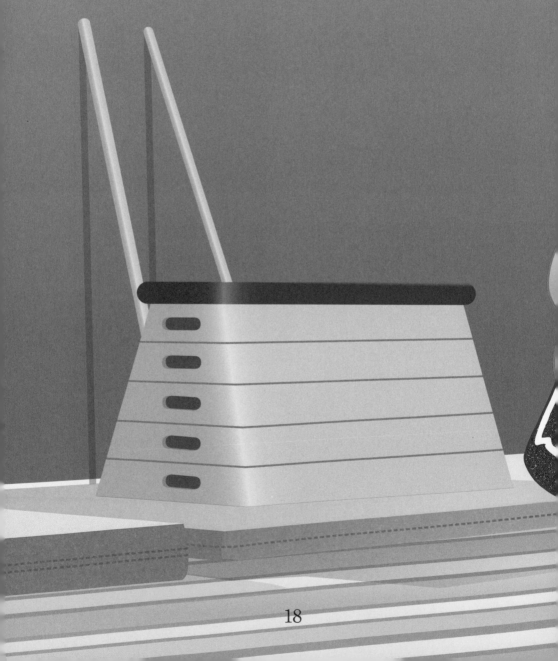

Barbie practices.

She jumps.

Coach Jenna helps her.

So does her team.

It's time
for the big meet!
Barbie leaps
with her
ribbon.

Barbie performs
on the beam.
She gets ready
to jump.

Her team knows
she can do it.

Barbie jumps.

She does a triple twist!

Barbie lands.

It's just right!

The judges give her

the highest score.

Barbie wins a gold medal!
Her team is so proud.
She thanks them
for all their help.

Thanks to teamwork,
Barbie can be
a gymnast!